D1558497

Barn Savers

by Linda Oatman High
Illustrated by Ted Lewin

BOYDS MILLS PRESS

The moon is a sliver of ice
melting in the sky
when Papa wakes me
for work.

I shiver as I dress:
soft flannel shirt,
long johns,
jeans,
hard hat,
boots,
and scratchy leather gloves.

We walk to Papa's truck,
slick from the melting moon,
and I pitch our lunch kettles in the back,
where Papa keeps his tools.

Finally, the darkness fades to dawn,
and the sun rolls before us
like a wagon wheel.

Soon we see the barn:
red paint peeling like sunburn,
and old boards, splintered with cracks.

Papa parks in the field
and I climb into the back
to fetch our lunch kettles,
two crowbars,
a sledgehammer,
and a rope.

I carry a crowbar and my lunch,
and we walk through weeds and
across a frosty field,
stubby with cornstalks.
"Look at that treasure," Papa whispers as we walk.
"And to think it all would have been wasted
if the bulldozers had come."

Papa saves barns from bulldozers.
"Is there a lot to save?" I ask.
Papa nods and I smile,
because I have a secret.
"What will we save?" I ask
as we go inside the barn,
the part that still stands.
"Everything," says Papa.

"Boards and beams,
joists and rafters and lightning rods,
flooring and siding and roofing,
windows and doors and the date stone that says 1893,
even this old pig trough."
Papa plops the tools in the trough,
and dust floats like chicken feed.
I sneeze, sniffing the barn smell of old hay and horses.

"Will we save that?" I ask,
pointing through the wrinkled, wavy window
to a weather vane horse
racing across a toppled pile of wood.
Papa nods.
"Your job is to stack the wood," he says.
"Watch out for nails."

I go outside,
where I stack and stack with my scratchy gloves,
careful of nails. I look at the weather vane
and think of how the horse once galloped
across the high roof of the barn,
twisting this way and that with the winds of long ago.

Papa comes out for lunchtime,
and we sit on the stacks,
eating sandwiches and drinking coffee.
"We'll recycle the whole barn," Papa says,
sipping his coffee.
"It'll sell like hot cakes:
people building barns,
people building houses,
people building houses to look like barns,
people fixing up barns for houses.
This barn will live for another hundred years,
in a hundred different places."
I nod, sipping my coffee slow like Papa.
"You're a good worker," Papa says.
"Time to go back to work."

I stack and stack, and the sun sinks low in the sky
like a sleepy, red-faced farmer.
Darkness falls soft and silent like chicken feathers
around the barn.
"Time to go home," Papa says.
I carry the crowbar and the weather vane horse.
This is my secret:
I'm saving something old, something from the barn,
for my new bedroom.

"It was a good day," Papa says
as we climb into the truck.
I nod, tired, the iron horse pressed cold against my cheek.

"I'm hungry as a bear," Papa says,
his voice raspy with dust,
as we pass barn after barn:
barns high and barns low,
barns old and barns new,
more barns for the barn savers to save.

For John—the Barn Saver—with gratitude
for support as solid as an old barn beam . . .
And for our barn-saving boys
      —LOH

For John High, with thanks
      —TL

Text copyright © 1999 by Linda Oatman High
Illustrations copyright © 1999 by Ted Lewin
All rights reserved
For information about permission to reproduce selections from this bo
please contact permissions@highlights.com.

Boyds Mills Press, Inc.
815 Church Street
Honesdale, Pennsylvania 18431
boydsmillspress.com
Printed in the United States of America

Publisher Cataloging-in-Publication Data
High, Linda Oatman.
   Barn Savers / by Linda Oatman High ; illustrated by Ted Lewin.-1st
edition.
   [32]p. : col. ill. ; cm.
Summary: A young boy helps his father recycle a 19th-century barn.
ISBN: 978-1-56397-403-8 (hc) • ISBN: 978-1-59078-964-3 (pb)
1. Barns—United States—History— Juvenile literature. 2. Barns—
United States—Conservation and restoration—Juvenile literature.
[1. Barns—United States—History.] I. Lewin, Ted, ill. II. Title.
 690/ .8922 —dc21   1999 CIP
Library of Congress Catalog Card Number 98-73068

First edition, 1999
The text of this book is set in Berkeley.
The illustrations are done in watercolor.

10 9 8 7 6 5 4